<u>NEMESIS</u>

BY

CHARLES DICKENS

British Library Cataloguing-in-Publication Data
A catalogue record for this book is available from
the British Library

Contents

CHARLES DICKENS

Charles John Huffam Dickens was born in Landport, Portsmouth in 1812. When he was ten years old, his family settled in Camden Town, a poor neighbourhood of London. A defining moment in the young Dickens' life came only two years later, when his father – the inspiration for the character of Mr Micawber in *David Copperfield* – was imprisoned in the Marshalsea debtor's prison. As a result, Dickens was sent to Warren's blacking factory, where he worked in appalling conditions and gained a first-hand acquaintance with poverty. After three years Dickens resumed his education, but the experience was highly formative for him, and would later be fictionalised in both *David Copperfield* and *Great Expectations*.

Dickens' writing career began in around 1830, when he started to write for the journals *The Mirror of Parliament* and *The True Sun*. Three years later, he became parliamentary journalist for *The Morning Chronicle*, and also began to have some successes with his fiction: His first short story, A 'Dinner at Popular Walk', appeared in the *Monthly Magazine* in December of 1833, and his first book, a collection titled *Sketches by Boz*, was published in 1836. However, his real breakthrough came in 1837, with the serialised publication of *Posthumous Papers of the Pickwick Club* – the work was hugely popular, and transformed Dickens into a well-known literary figure.

Over the next few years, at an almost incredible rate, Dickens wrote *Oliver Twist* (1837-39), *Nicholas Nickleby* (1838-39) and *The Old Curiosity Shop* and *Barnaby Rudge* (1840-41). In 1842, he travelled with his wife to the United States and Canada (where he gave lectures denouncing slavery), and in the years following produced his five 'Christmas Books'. During the fifties, after brief spells living in Italy and Switzerland, he continued to write at a seemingly inexhaustible pace, producing some of his best work: David Copperfield (1849-50), Bleak House (1852-53), Hard Times (1854), Little *Dorrit* (1857), *A Tale of Two Cities* (1859), and *Great Expectations* (1861).

During the latter stages of his life, Dickens turned his focus from writing to giving readings. In 1869, during one such reading, he collapsed, showing symptoms of a mild stroke. He died at home one year later, aged 58. He was buried in the Poets' Corner of Westminster Abbey, where the inscription on his tomb reads: "He was a sympathiser to the poor, the suffering, and the oppressed; and by his death, one of England's greatest writers is lost to the world." Dickens is now regarded as the greatest writer of the Victorian era, and one of the greatest English authors since Shakespeare.

Nemesis

The night had now come, when the old clerk Chuffey was to be delivered over to his keepers. In the midst of his guilty distractions, Jonas had not forgotten it.

It was a part of his guilty state of mind to remember it; for on his persistence in the scheme depended one of his precautions for his own safety. A hint, a word, from the old man, uttered at such a moment in attentive ears, might fire the train of suspicion, and destroy him. His watchfulness of every avenue by which the discovery of his guilt might be approached, sharpened with his sense of the danger by which he was encompassed. With murder on his soul, and its innumerable alarms and terrors dragging at him night and day, he would have repeated the crime, if he had seen a path of safety stretching out beyond. It was in his punishment; it was in his guilty condition. The very deed which his fears rendered insupportable, his fears would have impelled him to commit again.

But keeping the old man close, according to his design, would serve his turn. His purpose was to escape, when the first alarm and wonder had subsided: and when he could make the attempt without awakening instant suspicion. In the meanwhile these women would keep him quiet; and if the talking humour came upon him, would not be easily startled. He knew their trade.

Nor had he spoken idly when he said the old man should be gagged.

He had resolved to ensure his silence; and he looked to the end, not the means. He had been rough and rude and cruel to the old man all his life; and violence was natural to his mind in connexion with him. 'He shall be gagged if he speaks, and pinioned if he writes,' said Jonas, looking at him; for they sat alone together. 'He is mad enough for that; I'll go through with it!'

Hush!

Still listening! To every sound. He had listened ever since, and it had not come yet. The exposure of the Assurance office; the flight of Crimple and Bullamy with the plunder, and among the rest, as he feared, with his own bill, which he had not found in the pocket-book of the murdered man, and which with Mr Pecksniff's money had probably been remitted to one of other of those trusty friends for safe deposit at the banker's; his immense losses, and peril of being still called to account as a partner in the broken firm; all these things rose in his mind at one time and always, but he could not contemplate them. He was aware of their presence, and of the rage, discomfiture, and despair, they brought along with them; but he thought – of his own controlling power and direction he thought – of the one dread question only. When they would find the body in the wood.

He tried – he had never left off trying – not to forget it was there, for that was impossible, but to forget to weary himself by drawing vivid pictures of it in his fancy: by going softly about it and about it among the leaves, approaching it nearer and nearer through a gap in the boughs, and startling the very flies that were thickly sprinkled all over it, like heaps of dried currants. His mind was fixed and fastened on the discovery, for intelligence of which he listened intently to every cry and shout; listened when any one came in or went out; watched from the window the people who passed up and down the street; mistrusted his own looks and words. And the more his thoughts were set upon the discovery, the stronger was the fascination which attracted them to the thing itself: lying alone in the wood. He was for ever showing and presenting it, as it were, to every creature whom he saw. 'Look here! Do you know of this? Is it found? Do you suspect *me*?' If he had been condemned to bear the body in his arms, and lay it down for recognition at the feet of every one he met, it could not have been more constantly with him, or a cause of more monotonous and dismal occupation than it was in this state of his mind.

Still he was not sorry. It was no contrition or remorse for what he had done that moved him; it was nothing but alarm for his own security. The vague consciousness he possessed of having wrecked his fortune in the murderous venture, intensified his hatred and revenge, and made him set the greater store by what he had gained. The man was dead; nothing could undo that. He felt a triumph yet, in the reflection.

He had kept a jealous watch on Chuffey ever since the deed; seldom leaving him but on compulsion, and then for as short intervals as possible. They were alone together now. It was twilight, and the appointed time drew near at hand. Jonas walked up and down the room. The old man sat in his accustomed corner.

The slightest circumstance was matter of disquiet to the murderer, and he was made uneasy at this time by the absence of his wife, who had left home early in the afternoon, and had not returned yet. No tenderness for her was at the bottom of this; but he had a misgiving that she might have been waylaid, and tempted into saying something that would criminate him when the news came. For anything he knew, she might have knocked at the door of his room, while he was away, and discovered his plot. Confound her, it was like her pale face to be wandering up and down the house! Where was she now?

· 'She went to her good friend, Mrs Todgers,' said the old man, when he asked the question with an angry oath.

Aye! To be sure! Always stealing away into the company of that woman. She was no friend of his. Who could tell what devil's mischief they might hatch together! Let her be fetched home directly.

The old man, muttering some words softly, rose as if he would have gone himself, but Jonas thrust him back into his chair with an impatient imprecation, and sent a servant-girl to fetch her. When he had charged her with her errand he walked to and fro again, and never stopped till she came back, which she did pretty soon: the way being short, and the woman having made good haste.

Well! Where was she? Had she come?

No. She had left there, full three hours.

'Left there! Alone?'

The messenger had not asked; taking that for granted.

'Curse you for a fool. Bring candles!'

She had scarcely left the room when the old clerk, who had been unusually observant of him ever since he had asked about his wife, came suddenly upon him.

'Give her up!' cried the old man. 'Come! Give her up to me! Tell me what you have done with her. Quick! I have made no promises on that score. Tell me what you have done with her.'

He laid his hands upon his collar as he spoke, and grasped it: tightly too.

'You shall not leave me!' cried the old man. 'I am strong enough to cry out to the neighbours, and I will, unless you give her up. Give her up to me!'

Jonas was so dismayed and conscience-stricken, that he had not even hardihood enough to unclench the old man's hands with his own; but stood looking at him as well as he could in the darkness, without moving a finger. It was as much as he could do to ask him what he meant.

'I will know what you have done with her!' retorted Chuffey. 'If you hurt a hair of her head, you shall answer it. Poor thing! Poor thing! Where is she?'

'Why, you old madman!' said Jonas, in a low voice, and with trembling lips. 'What Bedlam fit has come upon you now?'

'It is enough to make me mad, seeing what I have seen in this house!' cried Chuffey. 'Where is my dear old master! Where is his only son that I have nursed upon my knee, a child! Where is she, she who was the last; she that I've seen pining day by day, and heard weeping in the dead of night! She was the last, the last of all my friends! Heaven help me, she was the very last!'

Seeing that the tears were stealing down his face, Jonas mustered courage to unclench his hands, and push him off before he answered:

'Did you hear me ask for her? Did you hear me send for her? How can I give you up what I haven't got, idiot! Ecod, I'd give her up to you and welcome, if I could; and a precious pair you'd be!'

'If she has come to any harm,' cried Chuffey, 'mind! I'm old and silly; but I have my memory sometimes; and if she has come to any harm —'

'Devil take you,' interrupted Jonas, but in a suppressed voice still; 'what harm do you suppose she has come to? I know no more where she is than you do; I wish I did. Wait till she comes home, and see; she can't be long. Will that content you?'

'Mind!' exclaimed the old man. 'Not a hair of her head! not a hair of her head ill-used! I won't bear it. I – I – have borne it too long, Jonas. I am silent, but I – I – I can speak. I – I – I can speak –' he stammered, as he crept back to his chair, and turned a threatening, though a feeble, look upon him.

'You can speak, can you!' thought Jonas. 'So, so, we'll stop your speaking. It's well I knew of this in good time. Prevention is better than cure.'

He had made a poor show of playing the bully and evincing a desire to conciliate at the same time, but was so afraid of the old man that great drops had started out upon his brown; and they stood there yet. His unusual tone of voice and agitated manner had sufficiently expressed his fear; but his face would have done so now, without that aid, as he again walked to and fro, glancing at him by the candle-light.

He stopped at the window to think. An opposite shop was lighted up; and the tradesman and a customer were reading some printed bill together across the counter. The sight brought him back, instantly, to the occupation he had forgotten. 'Look here! Do you know of this? Is it found? Do you suspect *me*?'

A hand upon the door. 'What's that!'

'A pleasant evenin',' said the voice of Mrs Gamp, 'though warm, which, bless you, Mr Chuzzlewit, we must expect when cowcumbers is three for twopence. How does Mr Chuffey find his self to-night, sir?'

Mrs Gamp kept particularly close to the door in saying this, and curtseyed more than usual. She did not appear to be quite so much at her ease as she generally was.

'Get him to his room,' said Jonas, walking up to her, and speaking in her ear. 'He has been raving to-night – stark mad. Don't talk while he's here, but come down again.'

'Poor sweet dear!' cried Mrs Gamp, with uncommon tenderness. 'He's all of a tremble.'

'Well he may be,' said Jonas, 'after the mad fit he has had. Get him up-stairs.'

She was by this time assisting him to rise.

'There's my blessed old chick!' cried Mrs Gamp, in a tone that was at once soothing and encouraging. 'There's my darlin' Mr Chuffey! Now come up to your own room, sir, and lay down on your bed a bit; for you're a-shakin' all over, as if your precious jints was hung upon wires. That's a good creetur! Come with Sairey!'

'Is she come home?' inquired the old man.

'She'll be here directly minnit,' returned Mrs Gamp. 'Come with Sairey, Mr Chuffey. Come with your own Sairey!'

The good woman had no reference to any female in the world in promising this speedy advent of the person for whom Mr Chuffey inquired, but merely threw it out as a means of pacifying the old man. It had its effect, for he permitted her to lead him away: and they quitted the room together.

Jonas looked out of the window again. They were still reading the printed paper in the shop opposite, and a third man had joined in the perusal. What could it be, to interest them so?

A dispute or discussion seemed to arise among them, for they all looked up from their reading together, and one of the three, who had been glancing over the shoulder of another, stepped back to explain or illustrate some action by his gestures.

Horror! How like the blow he had struck in the wood!

It beat him from the window as if it had lighted on himself. As he staggered into a chair he thought of the change in Mrs Gamp, exhibited in her new-born tenderness to her charge. Was that because it was found? – because she knew of it? – because she suspected him?

'Mr Chuffey is a-lyin' down,' said Mrs Gamp, returning, 'and much good may it do him, Mr Chuzzlewit, which harm it can't and good it may, be joyful!'

'Sit down,' said Jonas, hoarsely, 'and let us get this business done. Where is the other woman?'

'The other person's with him now,' she answered.

'That's right,' said Jonas. 'He is not fit to be left to himself. Why, he fastened on me to-night; here, upon my coat; like a savage dog. Old as he is, and feeble as he is usually, I had some trouble to shake him off. You – Hush! – It's nothing. You told me the other woman's name. I forget it.'

'I mentioned Betsey Prig,' said Mrs Gamp.

'She is to be trusted, is she?'

'That she ain't!' said Mrs Gamp; 'nor have I brought her, Mr Chuzzlewit. I've brought another, which engages to give every satigefaction.'

'What is her name?' asked Jonas.

Mrs Gamp looked at him in an odd way without returning any answer, but appeared to understand the question too.

'What is her name?' repeated Jonas.

'Her name,' said Mrs Gamp, 'is Harris.'

It was extraordinary how much effort it cost Mrs Gamp to pronounce the name she was commonly so ready with. She made some three or four gasps before she could get it out; and, when she had uttered it, pressed her hand upon her side, and turned up her eyes, as if she were going to faint away. But, knowing her to labour under a complication of internal disorders, which rendered a few drops of spirits indispensable at certain times to her existence, and which came on very strong when that remedy was not at hand, Jonas merely supposed her to be the victim of one of these attacks.

'Well!' he said, hastily, for he felt how incapable he was of confining his wandering attention to the subject. 'You and she have arranged to take care of him, have you?'

Mrs Gamp replied in the affirmative, and softly discharged herself of her familiar phrase, 'Turn and turn about; one off, one on.' But she spoke so tremulously that she felt called upon to add, 'which fiddle-strings is weakness to expredge my nerves this night!'

Jonas stopped to listen. Then said, hurriedly:

'We shall not quarrel about terms. Let them be the same as they were before. Keep him close, and keep him quiet. He must be restrained. He has got it in his head to-night that my wife's dead, and has been attacking me as if I had killed her. It's – it's common with mad people to take the worst fancies of those they like best. Isn't it?'

Mrs Gamp assented with a short groan.

'Keep him close, then, or in one of his fits he'll be doing me a mischief. And don't trust him at any time; for when he seems most rational, he's wildest in his talk. But that you know already. Let me see the other.'

'The t'other person, sir?' said Mrs Gamp.

'Aye! Go you to him and send the other. Quick! I'm busy.'

Mrs Gamp took two or three backward steps towards the door, and stopped there.

'It is your wishes, Mr Chuzzlewit,' she said, in a sort of quavering croak, 'to see the t'other person. Is it?'

But the ghastly change in Jonas told her that the other person was already seen. Before she could look round towards the door, she was put aside by old Martin's hand; and Chuffey and John Westlock entered with him.

'Let no one leave the house,' said Martin. 'This man is my brother's son. Ill-met, ill-trained, ill-begotten. If he moves from the spot on which he stands, or speaks a word above his breath to any person here, open the window, and call for help!'

'What right have you to give such directions in this house?' asked Jonas faintly.

'The right of your wrong-doing. Come in there!'

An irrepressible exclamation burst from the lips of Jonas, as Lewsome entered at the door. It was not a groan, or a shriek, or a word, but was wholly unlike any sound that had ever fallen on the ears of those who heard it, while at the same time it was the most sharp and terrible expression of what was working in his guilty breast, that nature could have invented.

He had done murder for this! He had girdled himself about with perils, agonies of mind, innumerable fears, for this! He had hidden his secret in the wood; pressed and stamped it down into the bloody ground; and here it started up when least expected, miles upon miles away; known to many; proclaiming itself from the lips of an old man who had renewed his strength and vigour as by a miracle, to give it voice against him!

He leaned his hand on the back of a chair, and looked at them. It was in vain to try to do so scornfully, or with his usual insolence. He required the chair for his support. But he made a struggle for it.

'I know that fellow,' he said, fetching his breath at every word, and pointing his trembling finger towards Lewsome. 'He's the greatest liar alive. What's his last tale? Ha, ha! You're rare fellows, too! Why, that uncle of mine is childish; he's even a greater child than his brother, my father, was, in his old age; or than Chuffey is. What the devil do you mean,' he added, looking fiercely at John Westlock and Mark Tapley (the latter had entered with Lewsome), 'by coming here, and bringing two idiots and a knave with you to take my house by storm? Hallo, there! Open the door! Turn these strangers out!'

'I tell you what,' cried Mr Tapley, coming forward, 'if it wasn't for your name, I'd drag you through the streets of my own accord, and single-handed, I would! Ah, I would! Don't try and look bold at me. You can't do it! Now go on, sir,' this was to old Martin. 'Bring the murderin' wagabond upon his knees! If he wants noise, he shall have enough of it; for as sure as he's a shiverin' from head to foot, I'll raise a uproar at this winder that shall bring half London in. Go on, sir! Let him try me once, and see whether I'm a man of my word or not.'

With that, Mark folded his arms, and took his seat upon the window-ledge, with an air of general preparation for anything, which seemed to imply that he was equally ready to jump out himself, or to throw Jonas out, upon receiving the slightest hint that it would be agreeable to the company.

Old Martin turned to Lewsome:

'This is the man,' he said, extending his hand towards Jonas. 'Is it?'

'You need do no more than look at him to be sure of that, or of the truth of what I have said,' was the reply. 'He is my witness.'

'Oh, brother!' cried old Martin, clasping his hands and lifting up his eyes. 'Oh, brother, brother! Were we strangers half our lives that you might breed a wretch like this, and I make life a desert by withering every flower that grew about me! Is it the natural end of your precepts and mine, that this should be the creature of your rearing, training, teaching, hoarding, striving for: and I the means of bringing him to punishment, when nothing can repair the wasted past!'

He sat down upon a chair as he spoke, and turning away his face, was silent for a few moments. Then with recovered energy he proceeded:

'But the accursed harvest of our mistaken lives shall be trodden down. It is not too late for that. You are confronted with this man, yon monster there; not to be spared, but to be dealt with justly. Hear what he says! Reply, be silent, contradict, repeat, defy, do what you please. My course will be the same. Go on! And you,' he said to Chuffey, 'for the love of your old friend, speak out, good fellow!'

'I have been silent for his love!' cried the old man. 'He urged me to it. He made me promise it upon his dying bed. I never would have spoken, but for your finding out so much. I have thought about it ever since: I couldn't help that: and sometimes I have had it all before me in a dream: but in the daytime, not in sleep. Is there such a kind of dream?' said Chuffey, looking anxiously in old Martin's face.

As Martin made him an encouraging reply, he listened attentively to his voice, and smiled.

'Ah, aye!' he cried. 'He often spoke to me like that. We were at school together, he and I. I couldn't turn against his son, you know – his only son, Mr Chuzzlewit!'

'I would to Heaven you had been his son!' said Martin.

'You speak so like my dear old master,' cried the old man with a childish delight, 'that I almost think I hear him. I can hear you quite as well as I used to hear him. It makes me young again. He never spoke unkindly to me, and I always understood him. I could always see him too, though my sight was dim. Well, well! He's dead, he's dead. He was very good to me, my dear old master!'

He shook his head mournfully over the brother's hand. At this moment Mark, who had been glancing out of the window, left the room.

'I couldn't turn against his only son, you know,' said Chuffey. 'He has nearly driven me to do it sometimes; he very nearly did to-night. Ah!' cried the old man, with a sudden recollection of the cause. 'Where is she? She's not come home!'

'Do you mean his wife?' said Mr Chuzzlewit.

'Yes.'

'I have removed her. She is in my care, and will be spared the present knowledge of what is passing here. She has known misery enough, without that addition.'

Jonas heard this with a sinking heart. He knew that they were on his heels, and felt that they were resolute to run him to destruction. Inch by inch the ground beneath him was sliding from his feet; faster and faster the encircling ruin contracted and contracted towards himself, its wicked centre, until it should close in and crush him.

And now he heard the voice of his accomplice stating to his face, with every circumstance of time and place and incident; and openly proclaiming, with no reserve, suppression, passion, or concealment; all the truth. The truth, which nothing would keep down; which blood would not smother, and earth would not hide; the truth, whose terrible

14

inspiration seemed to change dotards into strong men; and on whose avenging wings, one whom he had supposed to be at the extremest corner of the earth came swooping down upon him.

He tried to deny it, but his tongue would not move. He conceived some desperate thought of rushing away, and tearing through the streets; but his limbs would as little answer to his will as his stark, stiff, staring face. All this time the voice went slowly on, denouncing him. It was as if every drop of blood in the wood had found a voice to jeer him with.

When it ceased, another voice took up the tale, but strangely: for the old clerk, who had watched, and listened to the whole, and had wrung his hands from time to time, as if he knew its truth and could confirm it, broke in with these words:

'No, no, no! you're wrong; you're wrong – all wrong together! Have patience, for the truth is only known to me!'

'How can that be,' said his old master's brother, 'after what you have heard? Besides, you said just now, above-stairs, when I told you of the accusation against him, that you knew he was his father's murderer.'

'Aye, yes! and so he was!' cried Chuffey, wildly. 'But not as you suppose – not as you suppose. Stay! Give me a moment's time. I have it all here – all here! It was foul, foul, cruel, bad; but not as you suppose. Stay, stay!'

He put his hands up to his head, as if it throbbed or pained him. After looking about him in a wandering and vacant manner for some moments, his eyes rested upon Jonas, when they kindled up with sudden recollection and intelligence.

'Yes!' cried old Chuffey, 'yes! That's how it was. It's all upon me now. He – he got up from his bed before he died, to be sure, to say that he forgave him; and he came down with me into this room; and when he saw him – his only son, the son he loved – his speech forsook him: he had no speech for what he knew – and no one understood him except me. But I did – I did!'

Old Martin regarded him in amazement; so did his companions. Mrs Gamp, who had said nothing yet; but had kept two-thirds of herself behind the door, ready for escape, and one-third in the room, ready for siding with the strongest party; came a little further in and remarked, with a sob, that Mr Chuffey was 'the sweetest old creetur goin'.'

'He bought the stuff,' said Chuffey, stretching out his arm towards Jonas, while an unwonted fire shone in his eye, and lightened up his face; 'he bought the stuff, no doubt, as you have heard, and brought it home. He mixed the stuff – look at him! – with some sweetmeat in a jar, exactly as the medicine for his father's cough was mixed, and put it in a drawer; in that drawer yonder in the desk; he knows which drawer I mean! He kept it there locked up. But his courage failed him, or his heart was touched – my God! I hope it was his heart! He was his only son! – and he did not put it in the usual place, where my old master would have taken it twenty times a day.'

The trembling figure of the old man shook with the strong emotions that possessed him. But, with the same light in his eye, and with his arm outstretched, and with his grey hair stirring on his head, he seemed to grow in size, and was like a man inspired. Jonas shrunk from looking at him, and cowered down into the chair by which he had held. It seemed as if this tremendous Truth could make the dumb speak.

'I know it every word now!' cried Chuffey. 'Every word! He put it in that drawer, as I have said. He went so often there, and was so secret, that his father took notice of it; and when he was out, had it opened. We were there together, and we found the mixture – Mr Chuzzlewit and I. He took it into his possession, and made light of it at the time; but in the night he came to my bedside, weeping, and told me that his own son had it in his mind to poison him. "Oh, Chuff," he said, "oh, dear old Chuff! a voice came into my room to-night, and told me that this crime began with me. It began when I taught him to be too covetous of what I have to leave, and made the expectation of it his great business!" Those were his words; aye, they are his very words! If he was a hard man now and then, it was for his only son. He loved his only son, and he was always good to me!'

Jonas listened with increased attention. Hope was breaking in upon him.

' "He shall not weary for my death, Chuff:" that was what he said next,' pursued the old clerk, as he wiped his eyes; 'that was what he said next, crying like a little child: "He shall not weary for my death, Chuff. He shall have it now; he shall marry where he has a fancy, Chuff, although it don't please me; and you and I will go away and live upon a little. I always loved him; perhaps he'll love *me* then. It's a dreadful thing to have my own child thirsting for my death. But I might have known it. I have sown, and I must reap. He shall believe that I am taking this; and when I see that he is sorry, and has all he wants, I'll tell him that I found it out, and I'll forgive him. He'll make a better man of his own son, and be a better man himself, perhaps, Chuff!" '

Poor Chuffey paused to dry his eyes again. Old Martin's face was hidden in his hands. Jonas listened still more keenly, and his breast heaved like a swollen water, but with hope. With growing hope.

'My dear old master made believe next day,' said Chuffey, 'that he had opened the drawer by mistake with a key from the bunch, which happened to fit it (we had one made and hung upon it); and that he had been surprised to find his fresh supply of cough medicine in such a place, but supposed it had been put there in a hurry when the drawer stood open. We burnt it; but his son believed that he was taking it – he knows he did. Once Mr Chuzzlewit to try him took heart to say it had a strange taste; and he got up directly, and went out.'

Jonas gave a short, dry cough; and, changing his position for an easier one, folded his arms without looking at them, though they could now see his face.

'Mr Chuzzlewit wrote to her father; I mean the father of the poor thing who's his wife;' said Chuffey; 'and got him to come up: intending to hasten on the marriage. But his mind, like mine, went a little wrong through grief, and then his heart broke. He sank and altered from the time when he came to me in the night; and never held up his head again. It was only a few days, but he had never changed so much in twice the years. "Spare him, Chuff!" he said, before he died. They were the only words he could speak. "Spare him, Chuff!" I promised him I would. I've tried to do it. He's his only son.'

In his recollection of the last scene in his old friend's life, poor Chuffey's voice, which had grown weaker and weaker, quite deserted him. Making a motion with his hand, as if he would have said that Anthony had taken it, and had died with it in his, he retreated to the corner where he usually concealed his sorrows; and was silent.

Jonas could look at his company now, and vauntingly too. 'Well!' he said, after a pause. 'Are you satisfied? Or have you any more of your plots to broach? Why that fellow, Lewsome, can invent 'em for you by the score. Is this all? Have you nothing else?'

Old Martin looked at him steadily.

'Whether you are what you seemed to be at Pecksniff's, or are something else and a mountebank, I don't know and I don't care,' said Jonas, looking downward with a smile, 'but I don't want you here. You were here so often when your brother was alive, and were always so fond of him (your dear, dear brother, and you would have been cuffing one another before this, ecod!), that I am not surprised at your being attached to the place; but the place is not attached to you, and you can't leave it too soon, though you may leave it too late. And for my wife, old man, send her home straight, or it will be the worse for her. Ha, ha! You carry it with a high hand too! But it isn't hanging yet for a man to keep a penn'orth of poison for his own purposes, and have it taken from him by two old crazy jolter-heads who go and act a play about it. Ha, ha! Do you see the door?'

His base triumph, struggling with his cowardice, and shame, and guilt, was so detestable, that they turned away from him, as if he were some obscene and filthy animal, repugnant to the sight. And here that last black crime was busy with him too; working within him to his perdition. But for that, the old clerk's story might have touched him, though never so lightly; but for that, the sudden removal of so great a load might have brought about some wholesome change even in him. With that deed done, however; with that unnecessary wasteful danger haunting him; despair was in his very triumph and relief; wild, ungovernable, raging despair, for the uselessness of the peril into which he had plunged; despair that hardened him and maddened him, and set his teeth a-grinding in a moment of his exultation.

'My good friend!' said old Martin, laying his hand on Chuffey's sleeve. 'This is no place for you to remain in. Come with me.'

'Just his old way!' cried Chuffey, looking up into his face. 'I almost believe it's Mr Chuzzlewit alive again. Yes! Take me with you! Stay, though, stay.'

'For what?' asked old Martin.

'I can't leave her, poor thing!' said Chuffey. 'She has been very good to me. I can't leave her, Mr Chuzzlewit. Thank you kindly. I'll remain here. I hav'n't long to remain; it's no great matter.'

As he meekly shook his poor, grey head, and thanked old Martin in these words, Mrs Gamp, now entirely in the room, was affected to tears.

'The mercy as it is!' she said, 'as sech a dear, good, reverend creetur never got into the clutches of Betsey Prig, which but for me he would have done, undoubted, facts bein' stubborn and not easy drove!'

'You heard me speak to you just now, old man,' said Jonas to his uncle. 'I'll have no more tampering with my people, man or woman. Do you see the door?'

'Do *you* see the door?' returned the voice of Mark, coming from that direction. 'Look at it!'

He looked, and his gaze was nailed there. Fatal, ill-omened, blighted threshold, cursed by his father's footsteps in his dying hour, cursed by his young wife's sorrowing tread, cursed by the daily shadow of the old clerk's figure, cursed by the crossing of his murderer's feet – what men were standing in the doorway!

Nadgett foremost.

Hark! It came on, roaring like a sea! Hawkers burst into the street, crying it up and down; windows were thrown open that the inhabitants might hear it; people stopped to listen in the road and on the pavement; the bells, the same bells, began to ring: tumbling over one another in a dance of boisterous joy at the discovery (that was the sound they had in his distempered thoughts), and making their airy playground rock.

'That is the man,' said Nadgett. 'By the window!'

Three others came in, laid hands upon him, and secured him. It was so quickly done, that he had not lost sight of the informer's face for an instant when his wrists were manacled together.

'Murder,' said Nadgett, looking round on the astonished group. 'Let no one interfere.'

The sounding street repeated Murder; barbarous and dreadful Murder; Murder, Murder, Murder. Rolling on from house to house, and echoing from stone to stone, until the voices died away into the distant hum, which seemed to mutter the same word!

They all stood silent; listening, and gazing in each other's faces, as the noise passed on.

Old Martin was the first to speak, 'What terrible history is this?' he demanded.

'Ask *him*,' said Nadgett. 'You're his friend, sir. He can tell you, if he will. He knows more of it than I do, though I know much.'

'How do you know much?'

'I have not been watching him so long for nothing,' returned Nadgett. 'I never watched a man so close as I have watched him.'

Another of the phantom forms of this terrific Truth! Another of the many shapes in which it started up about him, out of vacancy. This man, of all men in the world, a spy upon him; this man, changing his identity: casting off his shrinking, purblind, unobservant character, and springing up into a watchful enemy! The dead man might have come out of the grave, and not confounded and appalled him more.

The game was up. The race was at an end; the rope was woven for his neck. If, by a miracle, he could escape from this strait, he had but to turn his face another way, no matter where, and there would rise some new avenger front to front with him; some infant in an hour grown old, or old man in an hour grown young, or blind man with his sight restored, or deaf man with his hearing given him. There was no chance. He sank down in a heap against the wall, and never hoped again from that moment.

'I am not his friend, although I have the dishonour to be his relative,' said Mr Chuzzlewit. 'You may speak to me. Where have you watched, and what have you seen?'

'I have watched in many places,' returned Nadgett, 'night and day. I have watched him lately, almost without rest or relief;' his anxious face and bloodshot eyes confirmed it. 'I little thought to what my watching was to lead. As little as he did when he slipped out in the night, dressed in those clothes which he afterwards sunk in a bundle at London Bridge!'

Jonas moved upon the ground like a man in bodily torture. He uttered a suppressed groan, as if he had been wounded by some cruel weapon; and plucked at the iron band upon his wrists, as though (his hands being free) he would have torn himself.

'Steady, kinsman!' said the chief officer of the party. 'Don't be violent.'

'Whom do you call kinsman?' asked old Martin sternly.

'You,' said the man, 'among others.'

Martin turned his scrutinising gaze upon him. He was sitting lazily across a chair with his arms resting on the back; eating nuts, and throwing the shells out of window as he cracked them; which he still continued to do while speaking.

'Aye,' he said, with a sulky nod. 'You may deny your nephews till you die, but Chevy Slyme is Chevy Slyme still, all the world over. Perhaps even you may feel it some disgrace to your own blood to be employed in this way. I'm to be bought off.'

'At every turn!' cried Martin, 'Self, self, self. Every one among them for himself!'

'You had better save one or two among them the trouble then, and be for them as well as *your*self,' replied his nephew. 'Look here at me! Can you see the man of your family who has more talent in his little finger than all the rest in their united brains, dressed as a police officer without being ashamed? I took up with this trade on purpose to shame you. I didn't think I should have to make a capture in the family, though.'

'If your debauchery, and that of your chosen friends, has really brought you to this level,' returned the old man, 'keep it. You are living honesty, I hope, and that's something.'

'Don't be hard upon my chosen friends,' returned Slyme, 'for they were sometimes your chosen friends too. Don't say you never employed my friend Tigg, for I know better. We quarrelled upon it.'

'I hired the fellow,' retorted Mr Chuzzlewit, 'and I paid him.'

'It's well you paid him,' said his nephew, 'for it would be too late to do so now. He has given his receipt in full – or had it forced from him rather.'

The old man looked at him as if he were curious to know what he meant, but scorned to prolong the conversation.

'I have always expected that he and I would be brought together again in the course of business,' said Slyme, taking a fresh handful of nuts from his pocket; 'but I thought he would be wanted for some swindling job; it never entered my head that I should hold a warrant for the apprehension of his murderer.'

'*His* murderer!' cried Mr Chuzzlewit, looking from one to another.

'His or Mr Montague's,' said Nadgett. 'They are the same, I am told. I accuse him yonder of the murder of Mr Montague, who was found last night, killed, in a wood. You will ask me why I accuse him, as you have already asked me how I know so much. I'll tell you. It can't remain a secret long.'

The ruling passion of the man expressed itself even then, in the tone of regret in which he deplored the approaching publicity of what he knew.

'I told you I had watched him,' he proceeded. 'I was instructed to do so by Mr Montague, in whose employment I have been for some time. We had our suspicions of him; and you know what they pointed at, for you have been discussing it since we have been waiting here, outside the room. If you care to hear now it's all over, in what our suspicions began, I'll tell you plainly: in a quarrel (it first came to our ears through a hint of his own) between him and another office in which his father's life was insured, and which had so much doubt and distrust upon the subject, that he compounded with them, and took half the money; and was glad to do it. Bit by bit, I ferreted out more cir-cumstances against him, and not a few. It required a little patience, but it's my calling. I found the nurse – here she is to confirm me; I found the doctor, I found the undertaker, I found the undertaker's man. I found out how the old gentleman there, Mr Chuffey, had behaved at the funeral; and I found out what this man,' touching Lewsome on the arm, 'had talked about in his fever. I found out how he conducted himself before his father's death, and how since, and how at the time; and writing it all down, and putting it carefully together, made case enough for Mr Montague to tax him with the crime, which (as he him-self believed until to-night) he had committed. I was by when this was done. You see him now. He is only worse than he was then.'

Oh, miserable, miserable fool! oh, insupportable, excruciating tor-ture! To find alive and active – a party to it all – the brain and right-hand of the secret he had thought to crush! In whom, though he had walled the murdered man up, by enchantment in a rock, the story would have lived and walked abroad ! He tried to stop his ears with his fettered arms, that he might shut out the rest.

As he crouched upon the floor, they drew away from him as if a pestilence were in his breath. They fell off, one by one, from that part of the room, leaving him alone upon the ground. Even those who had him in their keeping shunned him, and (with the exception of Slyme, who was still occupied with his nuts) kept apart.

'From that garret-window opposite,' said Nadgett, pointing across the narrow street, 'I have watched this house and him for days and nights. From that garret-window opposite I saw him return home, alone, from a journey on which he had set out with Mr Montague. That was my token that Mr Montague's end was gained; and I might rest easy

Mr Nadgett (at the rear) 'the first serious private detective in an English novel'. An illustration by Phiz for *Martin Chuzzlewit*

on my watch, though I was not to leave it until he dismissed me. But, standing at the door opposite, after dark, that same night, I saw a countryman steal out of this house, by a side-door in the court, who had never entered it. I knew his walk, and that it was himself, disguised. I followed him immediately. I lost him on the western road, still travelling westward.'

Jonas looked up at him for an instant, and muttered an oath.

'I could not comprehend what this meant,' said Nadgett: 'but, having seen so much, I resolved to see it out, and through. And I did. Learning, on inquiry at his house from his wife, that he was supposed to be sleeping in the room from which I had seen him go out, and that he had given strict orders not to be disturbed, I knew that he was coming back; and for his coming back I watched. I kept my watch in the street – in doorways, and such places – all that night; at the same window, all next day; and when night came on again, in the street once more. For I knew he would come back, as he had gone out, when this part of the town was empty. He did. Early in the morning, the same countryman came creeping, creeping, creeping home.'

'Look sharp!' interposed Slyme, who had now finished his nuts. 'This is quite irregular, Mr Nadgett.'

'I kept at the window all day,' said Nadgett, without heeding him. 'I think I never closed my eyes. At night, I saw him come out with a bundle. I followed him again. He went down the steps at London Bridge, and sunk it in the river. I now began to entertain some serious fears, and made a communication to the Police, which caused that bundle to be –'

'To be fished up,' interrupted Slyme. 'Be alive, Mr Nadgett.'

'It contained the dress I had seen him wear,' said Nadgett; 'stained with clay, and spotted with blood. Information of the murder was received in town last night. The wearer of that dress is already known to have been seen near the place; to have been lurking in that neighbourhood; and to have alighted from a coach coming from that part of the country, at a time exactly tallying with the very minute when I saw him returning home. The warrant has been out, and these officers have been with me, some hours. We chose our time; and seeing you come in, and seeing this person at the window –'

'Beckoned to him,' said Mark, taking up the thread of the narrative, on hearing this allusion to himself, 'to open the door; which he did with a deal of pleasure.'

'That's all at present,' said Nadgett, putting up his great pocket-book, which from mere habit he had produced when he began his revelation, and had kept in his hand all the time; 'but there is plenty more to come. You asked me for the facts, so far I have related them, and need not detain these gentlemen any longer. Are you ready, Mr Slyme?'

'And something more,' replied that worthy, rising. 'If you walk round to the office, we shall be there as soon as you. Tom! Get a coach!'